COLUMBIA COLLEGE LIBRARY
600 S. MICHIGAN AVENUE
CHICAGO, IL 60605

SEP 2 5 2009

EMILY WARN

The Novice Insomniac

COPPER CANYON PRESS

Copyright © 1996 by Emily Warn.

Publication of this book is supported by a grant from the National Endowment for the Arts and a grant from the Lannan Foundation. Additional support to Copper Canyon Press has been provided by the Andrew W. Mellon Foundation, the Lila Wallace–Reader's Digest Fund, and the Washington State Arts Commission. Copper Canyon Press is in residence with Centrum at Fort Worden State Park.

Library of Congress Cataloging-in-Publication Data
Warn, Emily.
The novice insomniac / by Emily Warn.
p. cm.
ISBN 1-55659-112-8 (pbk.)
I. Title.
PS3573.A763N68 1996
811'.54 – dc20   96-25194

COPPER CANYON PRESS
P.O. BOX 271, PORT TOWNSEND, WASHINGTON 98368

Acknowledgments

Grateful acknowledgment is made to Stanford University for a
Stegner Fellowship, to the Helene Wurlitzer Foundation of Taos,
New Mexico, for a residency, and to the Seattle Arts Commission
and King County Arts Commission & Landmarks Board for grants,
all of which allowed me to complete this book.

And to the editors of the following magazines in which some of
these poems first appeared:

The Arts
Blind Donkey
Backbone
Bridges
Calyx
Crab Creek Review
Cream City Review
Cut Bank
Hubbub
Kenyon Review
Limberlost Review
Mississippi Mud
Poetry East
Poetry Now
Rhino
River Styx
The Seattle Review
Southern Poetry Review
Willow Springs

I am also grateful to Denise Levertov, Sam Hamill, Chris Wiman,
Patricia Novotny, Carolyn Allen, and William O'Daly for their close
readings of this manuscript in its various forms. And to Daj Oberg,
Leah Fortin, Richard Irvine, Keith Geller, my mother Pearl Warn,
and all my other friends and family for their enduring support.

FOR ROSEMARY HARER

Contents

THE NOVICE INSOMNIAC

PART ONE

On the Insomniac's Watch

When insomniacs fall asleep after prolonged periods of sleep deprivation, their sleep is hallucinatory – a continual state of vivid dreaming during which they often believe themselves to be awake. Similarly, the waking state of insomniacs after a period of sleep deprivation is one of continual daydream.

– Esther Cohen, Sleep Expert

Moving

I wake in a strange room
    in a strange city
        delivering a funeral oration
or a lecture about rain.
    All day the dream bobs
        into view, sinks.

What combination of blown leaf
    and jangled light starts
        it talking?
If I could write down
    its instructions,
        I could fall in love,
find meaningful work.

Outside, rain drills its pointers
    into the ground,
        informs
the roots. Dirt clings.
Rain streaks like stars
    when a camera lens
        remains open all night.

Why do I insist
    on bronzing what vanishes?
To mimic rain's
    invisible circumference, change
as it does from silver points,
    to damp tunnels,

to the white ideographs
        of roots, to blank leaves
breathing rain back into the sky.

The Genesis of Insomnia

The wind gusts, hurtling small pines
against the fence. Hushes. I sulk.
I cannot drift into silence
or ribbons of dreams. The birds
start. I close the book of hours, rise
with the rising wind that breaks
the day out of night, the long night
with its absolute demarcations.

Nothing wings over my black desert
but Vegas. My calm stays distant
until we meet for breakfast
and roadside gambling. I have no
expectations, no routines,
no regular balanced meals.
Just this hunger to know how emptiness
formally unravels into fire, sea, dry land,
and yes, peaceable air. I kneel.
I ask the wind to seed my brain with sleep
so that I may build the rooms of God
then lounge in oblivion by the pool.

On the Insomniac's Watch

Down the block dogs howl
before the sirens wail, but after
a gunshot. Soon, a police car
prowls the hill and is gone.

Too late. Or no crime.
Just a woman shooting
at the hazy moon, at a pair
of sneakers looped over a wire.

Hiding in bushes, she hopes
they won't bring dogs.
She wants to cut through
the night's frozen fog, shatter it
as she did the silence.
Stars would fall through,
flakes of gold mica
on the gun barrel in her palms.

Porch lights bob
on dark waves of city hills.
Bushes scrape the house
against which she rests,
drifting on a warm sea

in an empty boat,
its wake a field of plowed stars.
She dips in her fingers.
Cat's eyes, ringed planets clink
and flash through her hands.

The Novice Insomniac

In her kitchen, she holds night
in a box. Inside, the moon drifts
and catches on shreds of clouds.
The clouds catch
    and slip through trees.
In their beds, sleepers do not count
the hours she holds them on her lap.
At four, wind. At five, moon sets in hills.
Sleepers scurry into cupboards.

In one corner, insomniacs
wrap string, sweep up
clipped moans, sighs.
Her helpers, they tidy streets
under shaggy pines, record
the hours of slate.
A stray car cruises one street,
then another. Stops.
A man gets out, knocks
on doors, kicks a garbage can.

Insomniacs glance up
from winding thoughts
into small boxes, from piling
the boxes by the curb. Please,
the man addresses them,
I cannot sleep. They shrug, point
to stars crowding the ceiling
for those few quick black hours
before dawn. Lights! Lights!

Tiny lights! She shakes the box,
stars spin, maintain their forms.
Dreams shine.

The Insomniac Ward

At dawn another insomniac stumbles in,
tired of tired, holding her head
in her hands, a spinning globe
on a demented axis. *Arrest*
my wobbling centrifugal whirl,
she pleads. *My dream lobe is awry.*

We cringe at another walking nimbus.
How insomniacs hate
their misfiring nervous systems,
malevolent maelstroms, colliding
molecules falsely aligned by the past.
We hold steady before their blank buzzing minds,
dispelling rumors of chimeras and shame.

Why are they so zingy?
Some have extra-sensory hearing,
sonar for rustlings and creaks;
others are brooders, intent
on their next mistake.

The dazed insomniacs stare
at the second hand of the clock,
another broken satellite, their job
to track its frozen orbit;
free will is a concept they shelve
next to the supernal realm
and self-esteem. Unbound text
scatters at their feet: misfiled hopes,
one-sided arguments, devotionals

to vacant selves, a discontinuous stream
of haywire memories that are hoarse
from shouting, from hailing the self,
mesmerized in front of our trick mirrors,
where they pull their faces into shape
for their hour-long stroll outside.

Rusted Hinge Bed and Breakfast

Above the boarded-up steps, a sign:
For Insomniacs and Memory Victims.
The maître d' offers me a trailer by a bent hayrake.

I ask to stay in the main house. The maître d' refuses.
(Someone watches from inside, waits.)
My manners, he mutters, prevent it.

A blue tarp billows on the plywood roof.
Socks dry, pinned to wire strung
around a sagging porch. Walls separate.

Has weather confined the watcher to one room?
Do mice and rain occupy the rest – windows
and doors multiplied by their gnawing?

If they can move between one world and the next....
Please, I beg the maître d', I must know
what is meant to be hidden. He shakes his head.

I stand in the yard surrounded by missing parts:
tractor seats, ceramic nodes, marsh hawk feathers.
I want to make them whole. Yet here everything decays into one.

What is inside the house? A desk and lamp?
A microscope with slides of spores?
Or rain-bitten plaster and a moldy chair?

I want an audience with the recluse. No trespassing.
Keep out. Go home, you homeless wanderer.
Must I instruct you how to dream?

PART TWO

Kaddish

Over the walk, sunflowers
droop their pocked, moony
faces, tired of it all.
But the bees despite
their tattered wings,
still lug pollen, love
their load – the weight
of desire made sacred
by denial.

– Gregory Orr

Encyclopedia

Each of us happens. Uninvited,
we arrive, checking out upholstery,
winking at grandparents finishing off life
with television. We prowl, famished, for a living,
read travel books, keep diaries, dream
until our minds resemble burning encyclopedias
hawked by a door-to-door salesman in Wyoming.

Over hot cups of ranch coffee he preaches:

>   Stores, he will sell you great stores
>   of knowledge: insect facts, dimensions
>   of pipe organs, remedies for distress
>   when pumps run dry or boots crack
>   in the cold. They could open on your table,
>   wait while you pitch hay to cattle
>   in shifting, howling snow, the white wind
>   a reminder of invitations issued at your births,
>   young men with fierce longings to stand apart
>   from families marked by silence and fear,
>   by hard work and the effort to be invisible.

The volumes A to Z arrive
at farm houses where mortgages
cannot be met. They are too weighty
to be true, too heavy for coincidence.
Fathers study their hands at kitchen tables,
unread, unschooled, while babies wail.

Icarus

A small child kneels
in the center of the room
while her parents argue.
She draws a picture of a house;
small, black v's of birds thin
into the whiteness of the paper sky.
The child feels herself disappearing;
soon she will be bodiless like the word
she cries into their sleep.
She cannot form the letters
in her mouth. Only in dream language
can she shade in her inheritance.

Kaddish

FOR MY FATHER

I bored through despair to find
a prairie of grief, wind at my back
and snow. How can I step across
the plain without him?

When we parted,
I stood in the train's doorway,
clutching my dress, hollering:
What if he never returns?

If only I had later asked:
what were we like
together? I ask now in memory,
entering the long tunnel
of the train crossing the prairie
and arrive at a station
where trains thunder in
and out. Is that him
on the bench hoping,
wild and stunned, for a glimpse
of me? I call to him
and hear the past repeating
its arrivals, instructions,
        departures.

California Poppy

I was crying for you.
You brought me a California poppy
in the scented warmth
under the eucalyptus.
You knelt beside me
and let your eyes be my eyes
to the bottom of the earth.
Was that the look we held
that later was no more?
A weight settled in me
as I became the person raised
without you. Come back,
moment in the grass.
Come back, momentary father.

Tracery

FOR S.V.M.

Yesterday it snowed like a furious
street musician peppering the ears
of guard dogs and footsteps
of criminals. Now darkness won't fall:
light from street lamps
    ricochets
between cloud cover and drift.

Memory can't restore what I lost
as you did when fresh snow fell
in the cemetery with its slanted graves,
their carved birds and engraved dates
no more to us than ornaments, an easy layer
of snow to scoop and throw at our gang
of college friends let out
    of cramped rooms by the storm.

We fought hard and furious. One boy,
in love with you too, stung me
with hard-fisted pellets. On returning
I learned that snow and cold had etched
a gravestone with my father's name.
He whom I never knew died
wandering home in winter,
his absence complete. You found me
in my room above the loud music
and jittery talk of a late night party.
Quietly, we rocked in the dark, the air
    thrumming
against the kettle drums of our ribs.

Eighteen

Lonely, I walked to where
   railroad tracks bridged gullies
      thick with fireweed.
All fall, I wandered the tracks
   or hitchhiked the roads, afraid
      of boxcars rattling past,
of men in cars who offered me rides.
One man grabbed my nipple,
   tugged hard
      as I shoved open the door.

All those girls who don't return,
who dream freedom in hollow ditches
   echoing
with blackbirds, who don't run
   into the brush far enough, into
      the pitiful shield of gorse bush
and highway pine, if only they knew,
   the rough arms of trees
      will hide them; their own hearts
pound a code animals know.
There are plenty of dried leaves
   and soft mounds of earth
that aren't young graves. I slept awhile,
   and then came home.

Litany

FOR A.G. AND C.G.

Her face after she sang them home was grief.
His face on hearing the singing was frozen white.
Her face and his face were wet with tears.
His face was drawn in an effort not to cry.
Her face and his face were red from crying.
His face was disbelief. Her face crumpled in her hands.
Her face was iron grey. When she sang them home
her face was sadness; her face was uplifted.
In those few moments while she sang,
we all ascended to where they must be listening.
We held them until the music stopped.
Then we held each other.
Then we faced the face of grief alone.

PART THREE

The House of Esther

Mordecai had this message delivered to Esther: "Do not imagine that you, of all the Jews, will escape with your life by being in the king's palace. On the contrary, if you keep silent in this crisis, relief and deliverance will come to the Jews from another quarter, while you and your father's house will perish. And who knows, perhaps you have attained to royal position for just such a crisis." Then Esther sent back this answer to Mordecai: "Go, assemble all the Jews who live in Shushan, and fast in my behalf; do not eat or drink for three days, night or day. I and my maidens will observe the same fast. Then I shall go to the king, though it is contrary to the law; and if I am to perish, I shall perish!"

– *The Book of Esther*
  (translated by the Jewish Publication Society)

There is doubt about the wisdom of speaking to God
Such labor could spin me forever, like a top.

– April Bernard, *Psalms*

Trouble

Began in pacing the Detroit desert
until I met Esther
pacing the other boundary.
She knew God. Praised
how I'd survived.
We compared manna.
Whatever you can imagine
as the laws require.
She knew them inside out
for each day of the week.
Without hiding her face,
she stared into the Shabbas flame,
tossed the Kiddish wine
into her mouth, celebrating
her rebel ways. And God,
she said, didn't blink.
Then I knew she was great as God
because her elaborate beautiful offerings
made her unafraid.
She is my hope and comfort.
She would laugh. Yet I know
she lived through God's terror
and doesn't take it lightly.
Nor my small fears that grow wide
and blank as the midwest sky.
Impossible to speak out.
But Esther does.
Then dances in her stocky
certain body, a kitchen dance,
careful not to break

the dishes or bang the pots,
but knowing if they break,
they break. I still cry out
when dogs bark
or floorboards creak.
And I sleep facing the door,
ready to greet God, the stranger.

Sounding the Good Name

Esther's name has lived five thousand years,
shouted under the desert stars with horns,
noisemakers, and paper furls. Esther lives
because each Esther turned toward the god
of the stars for a spell and each Esther
spelled the stars and each Esther stole
the god from the stars to survive
and each Esther lived in the heart
of every Esther and remembered
how many whispered thens and nows
and whens her name joined to the stars
risen from the lips of Esthers
crying their secret lot.
Oh when can she shake the stars with her laughter?

Esther "Etty" Hillesum broke
into the murderer's house, knowingly
asked to be transported to the death camps
so that her people could witness
an inner metal blind to an evil
as incomprehensible as God.

Esther "Etty" lives on in me,
in anyone who hears her name
and puzzles over the wind rushing
across it as across a barren space
of glittery stones and pines.
Listen to the wind rush through her.
Esther   Ishtar   Esthar
telling Esther's story.

The Rabbi Stumbles

The congregation watches stunned,
quiet for once, when the rabbi
loses his place in the Torah.

Nobody shifts in folding metal chairs.
No men bend inside prayer shawls to gossip.
No women comment about last night's Shabbas meal.

The rabbi is bending his head over the Torah
and weeping. A tear falls on the goat-skin parchment,
trailing across the Hebrew words like a rowboat's wake.

The congregation knows no law, no blessing,
for when a rabbi cries and cries and cannot speak.
Will his tears wash away the words of the Torah?

Will they erase the delicate balance between letter
and number? Did God whisper a saying in his ear
so holy it cannot be spoken?

Or does he see the blindness of all rabbis?
The congregation fidgets, then hears
its impatience and is ashamed.

The Torah cannot help them. The morning schedule
of prayers does not include his sorrow. They know
they cannot continue without a word from God.

The little girl watches the yellowish-orange light
falling through the cheap stained-glass windows.
She smells her grandfather's leathery tefilin;

the faint cigar smoke on his lips.
She reaches her hand into his roomy pockets,
feels their absolute comfort slipping away,

because the rabbi, a grown man, cannot stop crying.
In the silence, her grandfather knows the girl's place.

Tzaddik

Esther danced with the Hassids in Podalia,
with the tzaddiks in Minsk, with the rabbis in Koretz.
Esther studied Torah and Mishnah with them.
She laughed when they beat their breasts
on Yom Kippur. She laughed when Baal Shem Tov
and Rabbi Barukh and Rabbi Kobryn wept
at the end of their lives. She was their melancholy.
They yearned for her sweet intonation of the word.

Esther was every full moon, every unclean month,
    every birth of every girlchild.
She spoke the Torah's slippery words
    where no light glimmered.
She danced in the center of circles of Hassidic men.
She was their absence, their blindness,
    the holes in their moth-eaten prayer shawls,
the welts from the tight tefilin.
She was the Shekhina for whom they searched.

With Samson's Strength in Mind

I bow to my altar of scars,
white as lion bones
on my arm, each an icon
to violence
which first stirred in me
when schoolgirls taunted
my odd physical strength.
I could heft an ax,
split oak
easily as twigs.
The girls cast stones
at the seashore.
I mortared them into a pillar.
With cinders of star
I burned open my body
until I knew.

Walking past fishermen
on the city pier, I noticed
their barbed hooks,
the broken bottles,
the barnacles' razor mouths.
With them I could tear off
my carton of skin, sunder
what others threaten to maim,
my impulse inevitable
as the harbor buoy's
dong dong.
I hid among boulders
of the seawall

and whittled bones
on my skin
until blood appeared
and I licked it,
as when the skeleton
Samson left on the earth
broke into honey.

Rose

I caught my soul escaping.
This time I held on
as Esther watched from the armchair
as I floated free from words.
My body, gripped by the show,
knew neither catcalls nor applause
could stop the soul's pantomime.
With a razor I knew the answer,
how my body would bloom
and the spirit descend
to reenter the pain of the world.

I could not speak:
the house finch framed
by the window, the swish
of pine needles against granite
and my friends' crushed skulls.
How could I contain the breath of god
and the murderer's detachment,
contain the ghost of the mountain,
the pure white globe of the mountain
with its wispy beret of clouds
and the grey ashes of their bodies
drifting at the summit?

What can anchor me to earth,
to five thousand years of Jewish graves,
to authority in a random universe,
if not for Esther caring for my drifting
spirit, for my separated self.

How could I have found my way
back to my body, how could I hope
to be whole if not for Esther
containing my terror as I rose.

Procession

The day after I die
God appears in my backyard,
shakes his head,
can't find me anywhere.
Sniffs around the lilacs,
of course lilacs. It's spring
and I died young, died imitating Lincoln,
or Whitman who loved to plan his funeral.
God sees mine winding through the streets
with people waving esrogs and lulavs,
waving reeds and lemons behind my casket
crammed in a gardening truck with laurel hedge cuttings
and dug-up sod. It's on its way to the dump
leading a line of other junker gardening trucks
loaded with lawn mowers and rakes,
with grass clippings and crushed spring flowers:
tulips and rhodies, bleeding hearts and narcissi,
pansies and primroses, quince, lilac, apple
and cherry blossoms, the big saucers of the magnolias,
the cascading hair of the Aubretia...well,
probably mostly grass clippings and weeds,
of which I could list more than Whitman's catalogue
of smells, because I died and lived grubbing
that untamable, ragged, root-clenching crop.
That's why God can't find me.
I'm not in the casket or behind the lilac.
No heaven with its judgments for me.
No angelic robes or hell flames.
I'm a weed that springs up
just after you dig the last chickweed,

yank out the last dandelion,
a weed just beyond reach under the sword fern,
a weed with bottomless roots.
Give up on me God. Pick me and distill me
and turn me into wine. Get drunk on me, God,
because I'll last and last.

Raking the Gravel

All August, the empty lot fakes being a garden.
Pink and white sweet peas tangle in a trellis
of rusted wire, ripe pods swaying like wind chimes.
The blackberries ripen and nod above plumes
of dried grasses. And in the tough, spindly gorse bushes,
spiders string delicate nets to capture yellow flowers,
petals closed like the folded wings of moths.

Each morning I sit still here,
a stray cat in my cave of weeds,
and listen to Esther tell me
about the lot's higher purpose,
how it became holy by being quiet in the sun.
I don't believe her. But I want her to talk
as she does in August when all her gardens
rattle with flowers and gourds. I know she knows
my inner calm is dumb and blank from playing safe
with an old god. She used to doven like crazy, too,
she tells me. She'd rock back and forth
words looped together in a moan sent to heaven
like smoke from racetrack cigars.
No place, no thought, no hunger safe
from God's anger, unless she mouthed the lucky prayers.
She knew them all: the blessing for meat, for milk,
for fruit, for rain, for tears, for wine.
She wore sackcloth and ashes, shaved her head,
beat her breast, and turned her back
on summer to pray in the windowless synagogue.
And God, she said, never answered
like wind in the dried pods.

I sit there silent, letting Esther's words
clear a safe place in broken glass
and blackberry vines. She reads my silences
as first growth, thin grass that grows
after they cart off rubble and back-fill
the foundation with dirt. Soon, she promises,
I'll talk tough, thorny and bristled,
lush and clamoring as her tangled lot.

The Word Between the World and God

Which gods gave birth to which language?
Which language gave birth to which gods?
Which gods remembered which poems?
Which poems remembered which gods?
Which memory compelled the poet to write her first poem?
Which poem compelled the poet to remember her first memory?
Which memory broke into words without effort?
Which broken words were made whole by memory?
Which memory broke all the words in all the languages?
Which word unlocks the god hidden in the world?
Which hidden world contains the word of god?
Which hidden world have I locked away without words?
Which hidden world contains the ghost of a memory
too terrible for words?
Which words saved which souls?
Which souls gave which words to the world?
Which words said goodbye to which souls?
Which words are the last words?
Which words cross over the river of souls?

Who rescued herself with a word?
Who stole time for language?
Who encouraged language to steal?
Who taught language to be a sanctuary?
Who built a sanctuary out of words?
Who let herself listen to words hallowing the wind?
Who scooped out time in the quickening evening
by naming an eyeful of stars?

Her Boutique

The plants dream of flying southeast
in the window. Soon winter fogs and heating vents
will decorate the thin glass with mountain ranges.
Esther shakes a bracelet from a wooden bin.
The glass trinkets catch the light, focus her thoughts.
Today she means to clear a path to her table.
A little calm, an empty space
to sort through all those lives.
Soon they will arrive in small herds
looking for finds: pointed black shoes, sequined bags,
bubbled ashtrays – junk she cringes at selling.
They think she is a bargain;
they think they discovered her and her disordered shop,
her goods pilfered from Salvation Army bins.
They clamor for advice. How hard she works
to keep her spark alive. For years she has patched
their heirloom spoons, their wide-hipped lamps
with her chrome paint – exchanging one veneer for another,
so that she may sit in the back room,
empty except for a table and a lamp
to finish her story of the lost tribe.

Setting Celestial Signs on Terrestrial Beings

Creation is an emanation from the divine light; its
secret is not the coming into existence of something
new but the transmutation of the divine reality into
something defined and limited – into a world.

– Aldin Steinsaltz

I.

The angels laugh at Esther's folded wings.
Too much dust on the pocked earth,
they say. So much chaos of dried leaves
and newspapers piled in innumerable languages
always blowing away. No headlines
on our wrangling behind the scenes.

Esther laughs back, My kingdom opens on pines
and mourning doves singing on red slate tiles,
on jays squabbling, acorns in their beaks.

Ach, the angels say, too many potatoes,
the ants falling into your tea just
as the chanting begins. We offer you
an archangel position. No more sweeping up bugs.
You can be one of the flaming minyan,
spinning the planet on its greased spheres.

Esther says, No thanks, I like how sparrows
and two-year-olds can't stop babbling,
how they out-trill an avalanche of cars.
Most people can't hear you. Besides,
those who do are marked by distractedness.

II.

Esther opens her doors to bored angels,
tired of their one essence, of reflecting an above
and a below who want to learn the meaning of lost.

Earthbound, they remember the gate in the clouds
through which stars, moon, sun, wings,
clouds, leaves, rain, and snow hurtle.
They want to slip through trees like flocks
of sparrows. Esther teaches them to accept
what expands and contracts, as when rain stops
and collects in creeks. Muddy brown torrents
sweep away the slow gathering of dust after years
of drought. Clarity returns, rainwashed, windstripped.

III.

Esther welcomes exiles and prophets, grunge bands
and migrants, madwomen, merlins and psychics,
palm readers and punks, theologians who stare
into their tea cups, their intuitions crippled.

They bring her their unfinished prayers:
boxes of notebooks, paper scraps with God's
hyphenated names, an open book next to a potato grater.

Some need rungs, commas, and spikes,
need ladders, poles, cranes, and bricks, need slingshots,
rockets and wings. Some need silence. Others food.

Doubt assails Esther. Are broken prayers signs
of unmendable gods? With what chutzpah

does she think to finish them? No, not to finish,
to find and to listen, and in listening,
let them flow through her to their own unattainable ends.

Koan

Don't turn back
though you knock and knock
and cannot rouse Esther. She sleeps
or grates carrots and watches TV,
remembering the last salesman
with God on his breath
    and a pistol for witnessing
        this rough street.

Or she's lazy, staring at how wind
    tangos with a willow and slows,
        how the willow rests its head
            on the wind's shoulder and sways.
Just open the door with your credit card,
or silver toothpick, or sheer force.
Unlearn your manners. Forget whom you expect.
Then you will be with her watching the wind,
    ignoring the knock
        knock on the door.

Office Talk

All day long people talk to Esther,
while outside trees whisper with their many hands.
Some people talk quickly as leaves talk back to wind.
Others linger over stories, pull out snapshots.
One woman bites her lip as she speaks.
Another sighs. Supervisors' words intervene,
hurried words, panicked words. Something
is missing, something must be done. For awhile,
no one comes to talk. Fear narrows their throats.
Then Esther gestures wildly so the trees understand.

While the Secretaries Compose the Engineers' Torah

They want a chance at solitaire, the version played
on screen. They like the dealer's impersonal hum,
how he shuffles the blank display into flashing
diamonds and queens. The secretaries hope for a straight run
to five o'clock, a solid half-hour of good luck before
the boss intervenes or the fax scrolls out its orders.

All morning, the secretaries transcribe inspection reports:
the weather at 8 a.m. on November 10th – cloudy, cool
with sun breaks. The crew bolted the centrifugal pump
to the dry well, dug a biofiltration swale,
and covered the sewer line with native fill.
The secretaries dream with their headphones on
while the words fit into place: the water main
installation is fifty percent complete, the correct grade
achieved at such a such time on such a such date,
the feat inscribed in case the company stands accused
of design flaws, faulty procedures, or improperly cured cement.

The secretaries impatiently wait to exit Word
and enter the command for Dice. Perhaps today
they'll receive a stacked deck, a numerical sequence
to marvel at. They pray for no business until five,
when they can check out from checking out
the electronic dealer who arranges their cards.

The New Deal

Esther thinks about the hundreds
of little pigs that overran Chicago
in 1933, broke loose from the stockyards
where they'd been sent to protect
the price of bacon.
That same year mules trampled
cotton back into the fields,
fruit in California rotted,
while people starved.
Long lines of people moving west
made trails in the dust, like snails.
They left homesteads, family histories,
furniture on the side of the road.

Esther knows her place
reminds people of Hooverville.
Esther has a longer memory.
She wants children to pause
longer than the hiss of their taunts,
wants them to glue their eyes on marigolds
burning next to her picket fence.
When reporters come to write up her place
they give it a name: Natural Urban Household,
a slippery name in a culture
that depends on forgetting.
Her people taught her
    you shall never forget
    you shall never forget
calling the earth to witness.

Chrysanthemums

Esther brushes off the covers, startled
hard rain on the corrugated roof
hadn't roused her earlier, the autumn chill
in the room, damp enough to drink.
Lax, lazy, indolent, cold, she waits
until each dream resurfaces, flickers,
then folds into the steam of the kettle.
Would the world blossom if everyone paused
to decipher the thin veil of morning?
For this she works her garden beds
into a sign bright as Broadway lights.

She sniffs soot from last night's candles.
She worked late tracking the moon
by planting an arc of white chrysanthemums,
sweet frost flowers. She mixes ink
to sketch her plan for a winter garden
lush as a spring pond, marsh birds
motionless in wet greens rooted in mud.
The pond runs away forever
with wind and never leaves shore.
Her sketched waves cover the hard-pack
of her current city lot, bottle caps
and scrap iron ground into dirt.

Mid-morning, smog catches up with days
of clear weather, smudges her sketch.
Haze floats above the harbor, hangs
midway on the mountains like half-pulled blinds.
Helpless, she busies herself in the garden.

She collects seeds, snips dahlias, divides
yellow iris. Her garden will be like hills
rising in shades of blue out of the bay.

But the haze in the hills is not fog
or smoke from hermit fires. It is America breathing.
It is our driven selves, our clenched teeth,
the fast clip of radio news that drowns
silence and with it our ability to remember.
She remembers. She burns candles for the dead.
Their souls rise into chrysanthemum flowers.
Here, stand here, and breathe deeply.

PART FOUR

Highway Suite

Out of reluctant matter
What can be gathered?

– Czeslaw Milosz

Highway Suite

Leaving again,
my car drones up the pass,
drifts in and out of fog
before climbing steeply up
toward treeline.

Each time I travel through
the pass, a change occurs,
as the rain-fed,
rain-gorged,
lush green blossoming
of moss and mold gives way
to white slopes of snow.

It is like the moment
after I say goodbye.
We become ourselves
for a slow moment
I want to lengthen
between us.

The Map of Habits

You slow to register the ripple effect,
furrow water furrow as you drive
through Central Valley farm land,
past three tractors stalled in a brown winter field:
Egrets, still as dirt, poise on culverts
pouring muddy torrents into irrigation ditches,
where in clumps of wild grasses
and yellow mustard, you want to sleep.

Instead, you drift as you drive, tired
as earth under tractor cleats and spray
from giant orange moths. Weaving
between white lines, you coast
through Fresno, King City, Los Banos,
dream thread after dream thread tangling
with tail lights of leaves. The pompadour
of a bus driver. An empty rodeo. Migrants
huddled, waving at sparks flying
from a rusty barrel. A semi hustles by.
In the wind clap, ridge line pasted
on ridge line lifts off.
A plump hawk on a fence post salutes
        as you drive by.

Johnson's Orchards

In their tended order,
they are beautiful:
grafted from cultured stock,
shaped to hold sunlight
in their palms. Pewter-grey,
they cannot lose themselves
in the fog. They call to each other,
a slight clack of their clipped branches,
a slight tip of their frozen chalices
rippling up the perfect rows.

In the white dawn, a few yellow lights
spaced far apart on winter roads,
flick on; a few cars strafe the snow.
Soon the troops of pickups
and high school hotrods pass,
feeding the fog their headlights,
to work, to school, to swear
at the clock. But for a time,
under the brief coffee spell
in the cold front seat
the radio crackle warming the air,
we are free. Lulled by the hypnotic flash
of furrowed trees, we speed
past hayracks and stacked bins, past
apple trees which will outlast us,
rooted, sturdy, waving at the sky.

Rocky Mountain Novice

We drive into the Rockies,
late September golden light shines
in yellowing aspen. First stars float
above chiseled ridges.
   Night deepens.
The Milky Way is a long resting torso,
  star-filled, brimming.

In the morning,
  mammoth peaks radiate million-year-old warmth.
Each step up the dusty mountain quiets
our impulse to speak. We finish the day
in silence. Evening sun brushes grey cliffs
with rose light. The stove acts up.
I holler instructions. Shh your eyes say.
Don't disturb the quiet guest in your thoughts.

Wind gusts late in the night, a huge rush
out of silence, slapping the tent,
then collapses to a whisper of its larger voice.
The hard knots, points my mind hammers,
are boulders tossed by a slow-moving glacier.
Where they rest, water pools,
finds its course by spilling over forms
  that kept them still.

Everything guides the eye upward:
alpine fir and bear grass spires,
notched ladders of horsetails,
dried plumes of meadow grasses,

tiny mirrors of creek pools.
All attend the mountain's pure form.

In a dying autumn meadow,
the wind's cold stories shake all the firs.
Grasses quiver. Snow they think. Dead winter.
They bow when the wind rushes up the slope and is gone.

We stop for lunch on a flat rock,
a winding river far below glints
in deep green shag. Across the valley,
granite peaks tower, familiar giants
        after days of plodding.
Thoughts, which had been loud
        as deer hooves, stamp off
in dry meadows, easily shaken.

Beyond

I.

Far from the sea,
    seagulls cry
        flying over a small lake
in acres of wheat.
The fields slope up
    to rocky ridges
        where scattered pines
seem to count
    row after row
        of cloud trains
            coupling and uncoupling
in the blue yard.
    In the distance, a few
        spill their loads of rain.

II.

The horizon, not the sky,
draws me, the place where
the land's openness, and the sky's
endlessness meet. The sky shuffles
its tints and clouds. The land rustles.
The horizon stays put, a defining line
that recedes whenever I set out
to reach the notched boulder
on the farthest ridge.

III.

The lake shrinks in summer heat.
Mud flats appear. Geese land,
honk like old automobile horns,
then gun it and take off, banking
around the curve of the wheat bowl,
and gone. A lone sandhill crane
folds its long wings and settles on shore.

IV.

Too hot to move,
        I wait until dark
                to walk back through
moonlit ripe grain.
Ahead of me,
        on the dusty road,
                a porcupine bristles
its tail, then steps
        into the field, its body
                crashing and swaying

through stiff swaying wheat
which parts for it,
        then closes up
                and goes on whispering
about the sea.

Wind

For days, the word the wind shaped
in rye grass growing along the edge of fields
    eluded me.
Nor could I see what tips of wheat
sketched on the evening sky
    until I stopped believing
wind had anything other to say
    than wind:
wind in rye grass, wind
rattling dry sheaves,
wind in the walnut tree by the old homestead,
wind as constant as water
flowing through the single pipe
from the spring, incessant as the self asking,
    Who am I,
rattling down the roads with my blinders on?

Spring Visit

FOR PETER AND GEORGIA GOLDMARK

The yellow-headed blackbirds, rasping and sputtering,
perch on swaying cattails at their points on the pond.
The wind jostles their song in and out of hearing,
the shreee-eck fading with each heave of shore willows,
whose long strands buffet the gusts and hide cinnamon teals.

I row out to the wind-tossed island
and watch one long wave connect
the rippling wheat to the ruffled pond
to the blackbirds' guttural notes. The wild order
of wind, of swaying grasses and water,
seems utterly useless and certain of itself
surrounded by barns and the weathered henhouse,
the chickens pecking around hay bales, crowing
and clucking their domesticated song.

How do you bear such beauty?
Does the ceaseless activity of work –
of greasing a bearing on the combine,
or rounding up and feeding cattle,
or weeding shepherd's bane from the garden –
teach you to pause as the wind pauses,
teach you to be as ordinary as the teals
moving in and out of the reeds?

When your mother raised you here,
she paused only when snow or axle-deep mud
let her sit at her kitchen perch
and write back east about crop failures
and harvests, about frozen cattle and rural politics.

She wrote with an intensity equal to wind
driving snow against the house, as if to stamp
her name into the boulder-strewn, indifferent plateau.

Just before she died, she learned to rest
from her ordering of meals and family,
from books and ideas to wander
among her jumble of memories,
which bloomed like the leafless rock rose,
the first flower she named for you,
whose stubborn burst of petals returns
year after to year to bloom
among the lichen-covered rocks.

The shimmering orange sun slips
common as the blue stone mountains
in your kitchen window. In her last moments
your mother faced the emptiness of knowing
the world flows on without her,
that the pause between wind and silence,
between work and wonder, measures a breath
held between the living and the dead.

In California

Rain arrives in bursts
on steel drums of gutters.
Wind twirls hoop skirts
of garish yellow poplar leaves. Jays
fly through the sudden forest of drops
    loud as parrots.
After each storm cloud, an almost imperceptible
riff. Trees shake
a shower of coins.
The sky lightens. Spilled rain collects.
Then the drizzle begins,
    a faint buzz
that builds to a loud hush
answering a call
made yesterday by wind rushing through
brittle leaves, each a hollow gourd
the tree a marimba, saying water, water
until rain fell
popping off dry leaves
until only the living spoke
murmuring between storms,
a restless crowd between sets
impatient to be swinging hips
in one wild, luxuriant wave.

Topos

Nothing more than this held breath
    of meadow in spring sunlight,
bugs or is it white seed fluff
    drifting in and out of shadowy oak groves
through which I walk, bars of sunlight
    and knobby branches strapping me.

A rhythm begins, a loping forward
    along the rim of coastal hills,
thick impenetrable mat of oak
    and laurel below, cicada keening
in manzanita, in dry oak leaves
    and white grasses. A fury of pheasants,
a couple of deer edged out of hiding.

In an old orchard, a field of yellow mustard
    ablaze, tinder to half-dead trees,
        unpruned, useless, blooming.
Thoughts slow in the heat of the afternoon,
oak branches knocking after the wind dies.

I will pass the way of wood corrals,
wind dried or soaked with rain, horses rubbing
against them. I will pass the way of creeks in August,
thinning mirrors to the sky.

PART FIVE

Starvation Hill

It is the history of the idea of war that is beneath our other histories... But around and under and above it is another reality; like desert-water kept from the surface and the seed, like the old desert-answer needing its channels, the blessing of much work before it arrives to act and make flower. This history is the history of possibility.

– Muriel Rukeyser, *The Life of Poetry*

Starvation Hill

The last farm house is collapsing.
As it flattens into the slope,
it sinks first onto its back porch
as if sitting on its heels.
Its dark pupils stare at the sky.

Their blackness invites you to stare in
as people who lived here stared out.
Look through the empty door
to an apple tree outside the back window –
its panes long ago removed by a fist or a stone
or a swing of boards ripped from the house.

Walk down the busted stairwell to the basement,
lift the storage chest molding in the corner, searching
for hints of what was. Who papered the now-tattered roses
on the walls? Who scrubbed the floors, gouged now
with broken glass and thick with dust? Who sat
on the broad porch in the evenings, memorizing
the dusky purple of lilacs after returning home
from what work they could find?

A dog barks. Shimmy down the apple tree
and lie back in tall, cool grass. Sun bleaches the house,
collapsing into wet bottomland where sedges thrive.

Old Barn

Slightly, each day, it sinks
into the soggy pasture.
Whenever a gust
shimmies under its metal roof,
I hear horses neighing,
and sigh. How they butted
their heads against its rough-cut boards,
rubbing off flies and ticks.
How their knobby legs stamped
the puncheon floor of its stalls,
which smelled of horse breath
and manure, of hay squeezed
into the now echoing loft.

Back then wind rustled in corn stalks
Grandfather planted on its south side,
their leaves rubbing together
made a papery dry sound among
dripping cedars and ferns

Without their presences, I brood.
On my worst days, the wind
keeps its distance up the hillside,
rummaging in blackberry canes.
They do not gossip like willows
      or roar like old firs.

I could grow more calm
if I accepted the motorcycle parked
where horses stood, shop tools

hung neatly as hay bales,
light bulbs where lanterns glowed.
I could admire how its usefulness shifts
like shadows of the walnut tree
on its corrugated roof.

Community Hall Courtship, Vashon Island, 1945

There is something comforting in its whiteness,
the whiteness of chickens, of barnacles,
of low clouds above the wide grey Sound
along which he walks after feeding
his half-dozen cattle, after pulling thistle
from his acre of strawberries. He stares north:
pale silver flows between wings of forested shores.
A scattering of trawlers float,
    tetherless, nudging the flat sky.

He picks up a stone, grey and round
as every other on the rocky beach
and thinks how its smoothness
measures time. A killdeer cries, a motor
turns over, waves step on shore,
and he recalls the length of their embrace
last Saturday night on steps of the Community Hall,
her breath in his ear warm as wind
in blackberries, the uncut grass and daylilies brushing
his trousers, as other couples called out their goodbyes
walking down the road to their small farms.

Each voice moved through him,
carried him as the Sound buoys
fishing boats as they drift
on the swells. Now each time
he passes the Hall, driving his slow tractor
from one hay field to the next, he notices
the perfect shadow of its eaves, the porch
slightly off square, and its whiteness

becomes the moment when wind
mingled their goodbyes
with her breath, with the flit
of swallows harvesting the night air.
All of them in memory turn white, white
as ash, or sand, or salt tossed
in the sky and blown away.

Letter to Father from Beaumont Farm

When I see your hands again,
I will rest from speaking.
Their lines would be more deft than words
at telling how workhorses plowed pasture
for the first berry vines, the soil rich and dark
after your years as hired man on wheat ranches.

On days after you cut old canes and wrapped
new shoots around tight chicken wire,
I would pull tiny barbs from your thumbs' tough hide.
When my needle pierced your flesh,
you always shouted: You're going too deep!

After you died, the island felt empty
as the chicken houses you boarded up
when feed cost more than what you earned.
For months afterward, I would sit
on the dock at Lisabuela, the lights
of Olalla across the Western Passage
glimmering in the water like minnows.
The otter who lived under the old store
would surface ten yards out to say *shwet shwet*.

Every hour my new neighbors rush to town,
a far cry from when the Daily Needs Truck
stopped once a week, and Mother never purchased more
than flour or candy for every neighborhood child
who gathered round her stew pot, or skirmished
on the baseball diamond that you tamped out
of strawberry fields when skilled pickers disappeared.

All's not lost. By Wax Orchards, they sell flowers
on the honor system. Pick your bouquet of sweet peas,
daisies, and lilies. Leave your money under a stone.

I still grow your mixture of clover
in the south pasture. The same two bachelors swathe
and bale. When they finish, I serve apple-spice pie,
then they cart the hay to neighbors, a small gift
when I think of what you gave ferry riders
for your thirty years as deckhand; every dawn
your car loaded with boxes of apples
and pears, or burlap sacks full of squash.

How you lived instructs me and makes memory
a blessing, but your gift is the blessing
that has become my life, waking
day after day, season after season to light
sneaking across the pasture and under
Mother's lace curtains, to calls of hawks
above the open fields where you must be walking.

La Push Ocean Park

The Quileute woman we met had come to check
her gill net anchored to the spotted river rocks.
According to Quileute law, her net floated
one-third the width of the river, buoyed
by corks, held down by lead weights
and salmon caught in the netting.

Her family fished here for generations.
She named the men on the far side of river,
pointed out the tribal school (an old clapboard
Coast Guard Station), and the three fishhouses
where she sold her catch.
We peered in at the tribal center,
at its totems and Fisheries posters,
walked past dilapidated houses
and fixed-up quaint houses,
and muffler-dragging cars set against
a backdrop of sea and harbor mast.

The Quileute believe they die into an underworld
where they wait until spring to don salmon skins
and begin the yearly run past boulder and waterfall
to spawn. Human beings mirror nature,
beliefs that weave the living skein of the planet.
I wanted to ask that woman if she still believes.

Behind us, we heard the boom and lull of the sea.
Brown pelicans circled sea stacks.
Three children leaned out of her idling Chevrolet
laughing, impatient she took so long
telling strangers the price of salmon.

Place of the Salmon Weir

Salmon return to the hatchery for spawning in fall.
They come up through fish ladders and are kept in
holding ponds. The ripe salmon are selected for
spawning. They are separated male from female. The
selected salmon are killed for easy handling. The belly
of the females are cut open to release their eggs. The
eggs are fertilized by the male sperm. The spawned-
out carcasses are sold and made into pet food.

– From a Display Poster at the Washington State
Green River Fish Hatchery

Out of the nothing of sea,
that shifting grey-blue shadow of sky,
the salmon came, sequined, swift as milky
glacial creeks, species varied as local tides
and soils. Numerous as pollen. Adaptable to drought,
volcano ash, heating and cooling of ocean currents.
Survivors, changelings from fresh water to salt to fresh,
journeying in deep ocean currents, in surf, in river deltas
and rapids, leaping logjams, boulders, gravel bars,
knowing the moment to return, knowing the silky feel
of the one passageway on the long coast.

Above the concrete holding ponds, a kingfisher chatters,
flushed from scrub alder by my arrival. I wait.
Another appears. Together they patrol fish ladders,
diversion dams siphoning water from the river bend
that Puyallups named Place of the Barrier.
Here dog salmon and silvers, jumpbacks, steelheads,
and spring chinooks ran the ribbed waters of Soos Creek.
Behind the Visitor Center, a man restores a Fisheries logo
to a pickup truck. Stifling heat bakes the parking lot.
Late August; it's the wrong time of year for that salmon
carcass to rest on gravel in the shallow creek.

Puyallups built salmon weirs at river bends
where steep bluffs faced flat shores. With cedar bark,
they lashed tripods to span the river's width,
those on land tapping timbers with stones
to guide those working under water. Women wove
mats of sharpened firs and cedar branches,
an impenetrable wall held in place against timbers
by the current's force. From mid-afternoon through night,
all during spawning, Puyallups waited mid-river on planks
holding cords of pussy willow or nettle fiber to register
each tremor of salmon leaping the barrier into their nets.

The kingfishers' cries bolt through me.
Are they guarding the carcass on the gravel bar?
Or accompanying its soul back to sea? Are they telling
how Snoqualm named the jumpback salmon?
Or are the kingfishers hungry and tired of searching
for a way through the wire mesh
strung above the holding ponds where fingerlings
weave and flash churning the penned waters?

Fort Tilton – Indian Wars 1856

Representatives of four thousand Indians living along
then northern shores of Puget Sound agreed to sell
their title to two million acres and move to reservations
in return for $150,000 payable over twenty years in
usable goods. The translation [of the treaty] was made
not in the language of the individual tribes but in the
Jargon, a bastard tongue composed of about three
hundred words of Indian, English, and French
derivation and better suited to barter than precise
diplomacy.

– Murray Morgan (*Skid Road*)

While soldiers waited

    for hostiles to sweep over the Cascades,

    a timpani of rain fell on the river,

    fish jumped for gnats above eddies, pooling

    in front of their windowless stockade.

While soldiers waited

    they scattered leaves with rifle shots,

    drank whiskey, shuffled cards

    and replayed the attack

    that left eight settlers dead.

While soldiers waited

    the *Snohomish, Skokomish, Duwamish,*

    the *Muckleshoots, Queelewamish, Seawamish,*

    the *Snoqualmie, Sakequells, Scadgets,*

    the *Squinamish, Keekallis, Scoquachams,*

    the *Swimmish, Nooksacks,* and *Lummy* gathered

    to mull over their losses:

    eighty percent of their peoples dead from disease since 1775;

    Chief Leschi captured while sowing winter wheat;

    seventeen Nisquallies killed by militia;

    Settlers increasing from zero to 4,000 in nine years.

While soldiers waited
>snow deepened in the passes,
black ice glazed the alders,
the salmon people rolled over
in the grave of the river
while Snoqualm, the Changer,
began walking backward
to his original home,
unnaming stones,
unnaming deer and bluejay.

While Snoqualm walked
>cold rain people
and cold wind people
patched up their fight.
Beaver snuffed out fire
in roots of all trees.
Muskrat re-buried sod
under layers of current.

While Snoqualm walked,
>winter rains battered the fort.
The river rose, whispering
hundreds of unnaming stories,
recording each on bottom stones.

Stump House

A man cored through the trunk
with an adze and ax, burrowing
to prove up his claim. While chips
flew, bluejay came to visit, singing

> *Kai! Kai! Are you making*
> *the cedar stump into a reed?*
> *A horsetail? A tunnel*
> *for wind and rain? Are you*
> *digging for food?*

The man stooped in his damp cave
and gathered chips in his hands
as if scooping bottom stones
from a creek. He felt brief sun
on his face. His high-top boots
were damp from wet grass.
He was carving a number out
of the earth: 320 timbered acres
would be his. He swung his ax
as clouds formed over the Cascades.

> Blue jay sang: *Kai! Kai!*

> *I will show you the hole in the sky*
> *where wind first came through, where rocks*
> *and sky strike together and apart. I sailed*
> *up and down like your ax before darting in*
> *to rescue Moon. Still, Earth caught my head*
> *and made it flat. Once through, I sang*
> *with gladness: Kai! Kai! Kai!*

In the clearing, huckleberries ripened.
The man's palms blistered. Sweat poured
from the brim of his hat. He was hollowing
a home, a dry place where winds
would turn around. On Sunday he rested,
lying with his feet sticking out,
his eyes watching clouds cross through
the hole he had made. He wished
his stump were a living tree
and that he were a beetle tunneling
to the clouds that grazed the cedars,
instead of a man clearing brush from the land
to claim his happiness, to lie on it
and remember what had just lived there.

PART SIX

Bravura

becoming the wife of my beloved she was
carried to my father the impossible world is
all around us indistinguishably
one is this act the cause can be
anywhere

– Olga Broumas & T Begley
  Sappho's Gymnasium

Slow Awakening

I wake inside a fire-scarred redwood,
my face dusty with smoke
    of receding dreams.
I crossed the borderland with her,
    although far away.
How slowly Esther taught me
to fold myself within the trunk's rootedness.

Her bolt out
of summer's blue
became a brief foundry
of pine cones and needles
that flared and smoldered,
unraveling braided ropes of bark,
a fluid chisel, the sweet shavings
of smoke rising as faithfully
as spires rose, muscled stone
by muscled stone, following
the same curved space as a hearth,
or a seed pod broken open,
the wind fanning the flames
just enough to burn
the wet pith, to singe
the lower fronds;
the wetness of living wood,
the heat of fire branding
the tree with emptiness.

After Starting a Forest Fire

While we lay in the sun,
    upriver in the place of the deer,
the flames licked at the puzzle-bark of ponderosa pines,
    at the junipers and prickly pear cactus,
    at the scattered pine cones,
        each becoming a small mound of ash.
The flames sifted and devoured the soft grey ears of sage,
    each plant a burning bush,
    the hillside a minyan of spiraling smoke.
The wind rose wailing and hushing itself,
fueling the fire in last year's pale white grasses,
    which moments before had swayed and stirred
        in their ragged green wells.
The old and new gone now into white flakes
    smothering the air,
    their birth nests black.

Live, earth,
live in me,
    in him.
Live in the resurrected grass,
in the burst seed and snake.
Live in the waxy red cactus flowers
    in their burrows of rock,
in the wasp burying himself
    in their pollen.
Live in the pale blue moth
sipping the white wine of stream daisies,
in the dippers bobbing on the river boulders.
Live in the isthmus of the rivers' confluence
where we made our camp.

Live in us, earth,
in our hands that made the fire
that scorched a part of you:
     a basin of stone,
     a floor of soft needles and grass,
where we lay kindling you, a fiery loving god,
who burned and smoldered unnoticed
long after our bodies were warm.

We sit in the blackened earth,
     listening for you,
     each word a sounding.
The singed pines, straining to be born,
roam the air in the slightest wind.

Teach us how to reach like them in blessing
of this scarred but still living shelter,
where we lived inside each other,
the harmonic of two rivers converging,
     of silver sticks burning,
     a wild fire,
     out of which we came
     wholly consumed and new.

Bravura

Each day I learn
a few low notes,
a throbbing in my throat
an impulsive greeting.
Not to summon you,
but to call out
in extraordinary language
    here.

The high air, our striving,
made a reedy tune:
silence mixed with small bird cries
in the tallest pines.
We stopped to listen,
the same wind in our throats.

Why, when I think
of touching you,
does sadness weigh me?
And yet the same ache
urges me to sing with you
the one song that mends.

Axis Mundi

Like the thick trunk
in the steep ravine's wild mat
of salmonberry and fern,
we dug in to keep from sliding
into the creek as wet
as our hair streaming with rain,
mingling with sweat on our faces
as we lugged split wood up
the mud path from the alder,
which had towered, its branches
a center to wind, until my saw
whirred through and its trunk spun
on its last shred of bark and fell
into a cushion of humus and vine.

We clambered over
the fallen spire, split
the long trunk, clambered up,
slipped down, split the rounds,
cradled them close.

Just after dusk we ceased work,
the mist white as our skin,
whiter in the dark trees
and underbrush. The mist filled
the clearing where the goats sleep.
Brimmed. Brimming. We paused to be
with the goats, the leaves
sifting, the mist dripping,
patter of chicken feet,
our hands in the goats' tough fur,
almost dark, the mist softening

the dark woods, softening
our white skin. Later we would touch,
revive that moment breathing
the same rain, but not then,
then we stooped in the goat shed
watching how the clearing we broke out
of the woods held the wet sky,
like a cupped palm, or like a rock
that has been rounded, scooped
by rain falling, slowly carving
a basin where the animals can drink
from the net of rain we love.

The New Year

Which crow scolded me
about the bronze dawn I missed
while I lay dreaming of walking past
your house. I wanted you to glance out
your window, but my new partner hollered
to hurry. We might miss
the amber poplar leaves letting go
into quick flights, fluttering,
rocking back and forth until they burrow
into piles of leaves – hands laid on top
of hands, or ears pressed to the ground
to hear the giant machine created out
of the earth that I join when I rise to work,
my soul replaced by routine. I glide in the shell
of my car, one bead in a necklace of car lights
commuting across the pastel blue lake, the tips
of mountains lost in a grey wash of clouds.
The silver path of an almost absent sun, shimmering
and sashaying on the lake's grey surface, dares me
to ask the question that has no answer,
but is answered when I stop in place and look
at hillsides of roasted leaves: frosted oranges,
burnt sands, siennas, taupes, and beiges. Or when
I hear the wind in the dying trees shoo shooing,
whispering and humming a toneless sound, a multitude
of breaths held all summer and released, delicious
as flan, caramel, or cider. The hush moving up
and down, in and out, like frost or fire,
smoke or ice, one stirred alive, kindled
by my breath, the other rising into steam.

Regret

Blackbirds cluck in empty grass sheaves
as rain falls into flat brown land by the river.
I could say the blackbirds are bells,
but they are no more bells
than the snare drum of trucks
rounding the highway curve in the rain,
than sheep bleating in the hills,
than someone shifting in a chair,
     than her eyes.

I should lower mine.
When I look one too many times,
I know I have not yet learned to float
in my own emptiness. I should ask her name.
Blackbirds rise and disappear
into grasses, sheep call,
inviolably passing into dusk:
     singular, startling, absences.

Insomniac Rock

Your heart beats fast
as taxi fare
when you wake at three
thinking of her.
Just rock to it.
Snap the lights on. Sing.
Revel in cracked nights. Revel
in dazed dawns, in all-day REM,
while you wait to see her.
Maybe she's a chance
to sway a moment. To stop
your critique. Laugh
when she mimics and mimes.
When she two steps,
swing with her lankiness. Grimace
when she sends wry looks
of furrowed consternation.
Flirt, flatter, cajole.
Slip notes into her tight jeans:
I lie awake at night
because my eyes know yours.
My hands can explain.

Detained by Her Swagger I Miss a Deadline with Myself

We missed the cutoff
on our first walk in Berkeley hills
where the fireroad climbs past
    the eucalyptus grove.

I'm in a flurry, dusting off
my glass collection, folding
and refolding clothes,
rewinding arias. When can I ask
for love? Earlier applications
restrain me. I flirt instead.

When conversation lags,
she asks, What's your point?
To get her into bed.
But is it? Waiting
for her call, I am missing.
I am alive. Just as after the squall,
faded dry leaves appeared gold
in the sun, as gold as clock hands
inching toward her arrival.

Perhaps she's as nervous as I am
of losing bits and pieces, of flying
apart as when wind flung
eucalyptus leaves, spider duff,
old rain in our faces
as we walked, not willing
to stop though our ears burned
    with cold.

Parting, perhaps
she worked as hard
as I did, a mailbag slung
over my shoulder,
a thousand postcards to sort,
each one a remembered dart of her eyes.

The Flowering Branches

I cut a tangle of quince
its coral buds shielded
    by white-green petals.

In a hurry to see you
I left the vase behind
and arrived early
    your door locked
        hallway dim.

I stood where you would not see me
    and my armload of flowers
and clipped dead or leafy twigs
    from those about to bloom
arranged their heights
    to protect what I offered.

The stairwell door creaked. Keys jangled.
    I stepped out. You stared
at me at the flowers and smiled.
I'll check for a vase later you said. Let's talk.
I laid the sticks in a jumble on your desk.

Did you find a vase? Did you fill it with water?
Did you admire how the quince burst
    into vermilion?

PART SEVEN

Solitary Date Orchard

Wonder or radical amazement, the state of maladjustment to words and notions, is a prerequisite for an authentic awareness of that which is.

– Abraham Heschel, *The Prophets*

Evening Prayer

I taste the bitterness
    of acorns. I drink rain
        gathered in spoons
of live-oak leaves.
Am I walking toward you?

Fog spreads its white shadows
    over dark green coastal hills.
I climb a glazed path to where oaks,
    half-living, half-dead,
        tip toward the sea.

I rest my back against a blighted oak.
Mounds of clouds and hills change places slowly.
Behind me is an unseen door,
    a deep gash,
        from fire or rot.
Bees fly in and out,
    a slight crowd waiting
        to enter one by one.

The bees are a living stone
    rolling in front of a cave
        guarding the way.

Solitary Date Orchard

Yes, I wrestled
with pillars of light,
of dust. Yes, I solved
oracles, proverbs, parables.
A bell rings in a palm tree.
(I am not making this up.)
I climb into its nub,
sit under ribbed green fronds
that sift through trinkets
the wind hoists. Iridescent
pigeon feathers, eucalyptus quills
land in my lap. I spill my gleanings
into the roses, scattered seeds.
Who needs angel blessings,
the obedience clause
in fine print? Why work
at descendants? Soon people
will outnumber pollen.
Just this digit of earth,
this slow pendulum ride,
swinging from shadow
to light to shadow,
this small plot hatching
Egyptian bottle flies,
red ants, Anna's hummingbirds.
No chiseled covenants. No fixed source.

Maple Nebula

I can see now,
inside the factory of the sun,
inside wheels of leaves.

From moss I learned to steal light
from rivers, from rain, from clouds,
to creep along vine maples,
    advancing by absorbing
the molten green burn of leaves
until I grew thick enough
    to withstand
the blast furnace of light,
to live in the center of the whirl
    and beam.

Labor Day

A slight breeze nods the boats – drifting
pontoons on the bay. On the shore
we are just as lazy, stationed
on the grass for the best view.
We read novels, picnic to bury
our goals before autumn begins.

If I glance at waves
lapping the hulls, I am back
outside Detroit, the shallows littered
with rusty pipes that we empty
looking for crayfish or frogs.
We circle the shore, swim under piers,
chase the glint of sunfish, shells,
anything that lets us endlessly search
like minnows gleaming in and out of the weeds.
When we come to an opening,
where the breakwater has cracked,
where water crawls on shore and rests,
we rest, then explore further
until hunger forces us home.

Today, I forget the momentum of years,
and I am as yet unformed, faceless
as the girl who drifted along the shore
unaware the days shifted away from the sun.

Savings

I save my tears for you:
    slippery gems dug from a dry creek.

I store them
    in an empty spice jar,
    smelling of lemons pierced with cloves.

Please, open the lid
    when I am not there.
Then they will talk,
    spilling out,
    rattling the past.

Gather them in your hands
    and put them in your purse
    and pockets.
Then walk down my street,
    past the blackberries
    that snag your shirt,
    to my front door.

Open it and come in.
    Walk to where I sit,
    stiff and silent in the kitchen,
and pour the tears back into my eyes
until they glitter with life.

Practice

I can't contain the happiness I found
among cattails in a marsh
where waves practice sliding silver
    under lily pads.

Nor can I compete with the wren
singing its mad rain song in the river birch,
with the chef compiling her grocery list:
    three bunches of basil,
    freshly snapped green beans,
    garlic, pine nuts, parmesan cheese.

Everyday happiness slides through me
    and is gone,
like the wren's song in the trees,
waves flattening on shore,
pesto spooned on pasta and devoured.

Yet leaves absorb the wren's note
    and become more green.
The waves coax water lilies to open.
And these words, these bits
    of garlic and basil, taste
        of what I can offer.

Lost

I returned to where I first saw egrets,
white vases in the brown marsh. They stood,
as then, in constant bay wind, knee deep
in salt water, shying along grassy banks
or freezing in bent poses, ignoring coots
who clumsily chased each other.

I walked, wind in my face, out to the tip
of the marsh. Egrets shone like opals
against blue water and knuckles
of small green islands. They waded
shallows of mud flats, where seagulls
huddled in their mounds of feathers, perched
on top of rippled mounds of sand and pools
of water. Grey on grey on grey. Mud, water
and birds, each with their own sheen, together
a canvas of humped backs, the devoted
at their tasks. The light of dusk vanished
from the water. I heard an egret's soft call slide
into silence and then more distant calls echo,
reverberating up and down the coast, beyond
the reach of each bird's range.

Before Ordering the Day

Empty poplar branches hold the sun
this morning, a shimmering disc behind the fog,
a thick white plate from a breakfast diner,
its scratches buffed from years of use.

It pauses in the outstretched tips just
as the waitress fills my cup with coffee.
What would you like today?
Then gives me time to answer.

The bustle starts, she slaps down
my food and rushes off to take an order.
The sun climbs branch by branch until it clears
the top, dispersing fog. For a moment the fog resists,

spreads out a diffuse pink light that becomes backdrop
to each peaked roof, each flowering tree,
joined yet distinct. I taste a slice of orange with parsley,
     sip fresh black coffee.

New World Parrot

The locust tree, fluttery
with sunlight, wind,
is the same yellow-green as the lost
parrot who perches, unknown
to us, in your unmanageable
back yard, its row of dying
apple trees and lawn too large
to ever mow sunken below
the street. To cope, you planted
a circle of hostas, a nickel
of order around which we sip
champagne. Happy Birthday!
We whistle while you pull gifts
from a bag, a wind-up cow,
an Etch-A-Sketch key ring,
cards of Weimaraners and
crying babies. A young man waves
from the street. We wave
back, amused that people
walking by become bystanders
to our party of mostly women,
suntanned, chattering, some
brushing against, some kissing
each other, still
slightly risqué, so that when he
shouts politely that he has lost
his parrot has anyone seen
it, we shake our heads no,
laughing in unison except
one woman hollers, There! There!
pointing to a backlit

apple tree. Where?
we clamor, We can't see it.
as he climbs down the rockery
and the parrot swoops
into our party, landing
on a woman's shoulder
who stays still in the hubbub
until the man pulls
from his shirt pocket the bird's
favorite food. It curls
its claws around his finger and eats
and eats while the man sits
with us for the longest time
and tells us from the beginning
how the parrot flew
from its cage to join us.

Felon

In the eastern window
a woodpecker tests
a metal clothesline pole.
Its long thin beak samples
to the right, to the left,
as if to say, here I am,
a flasher, its only purpose
to shock me
into acknowledging
the invisible seam
between one being
and the next.

Flicker

Each time mourning doves flap up
to the birdfeeder, the flicker lifts
its black bead eyes to heaven.
It has found a stump, sawed off
close to the ground, the bark
black with age and rain,
split with fissures and cracks.

It lowers itself down
the trunk, its maniacal claws
splayed out on either side
of its plump spotted body.

Near the base, it leaps,
scuffles the dry leaves
and swivels its head,
surreptitiously,
before burying its beak
in rotten wood.

In rapid loud bursts,
it widens holes,
wedges open cracks,
sweeps out dust,
and occasionally grazes
on a beetle or centipede,
eyes gazing upward, wary
of cats' paws, hawks, or the dull,
mechanical flap of doves,

gorging themselves at the feeder,
a sustenance without effort
or delight in prying open
the tree's thick casket.

After Reading the Book of Splendor

A cloud hides the sun. A photograph
of a weathered boathouse on an empty beach
illumines the room. It has become itself over time,
sitting slightly off-square, hunched
over its vacant slip. Patches of moss
slant like rain on the steep shake roof.
The boathouse casts a shadow on the white sand
that is a door, a place for the eye to rest
after staring at the brightness
of the blank sky. Its other door never shuts.
It waits before the sea for the old wooden lorries
to return. There are no boats on the waves. No kelp
or driftwood on the beach. Just the boathouse,
doors unlatched.

Fog

One day I will become fog
and drift through spring trees
        half in petal half in leaf.
I will become the neighborhood,
assuming outlines of trees and bungalows
as grass assumes the broken ground
of a bulldozed lot. I will clothe
the body of the earth, the grey factory
and the blossoming magnolia
alike in their solitary communion with me.

I will return what fog gave me
in the years of my despair,
how I would sink into it
until my spirits rose out
of the half-hidden branches,
lifting as the fog lifted, returning
the world to itself as a gift.

Tower of Babel

After days, the torrential rains
stop. Clouds loiter in a tidy sky.
Fallen behind, they give up and dissolve.

I find a pine with step-ladder branches.
From the top rung I hear
    wind scattering original language.
All day I listen as it lifts words,
      feeds them to crows,
          and worries leaves with messages.

To gather scattered clans,
our ancestors flung their name
among stars – a fleeting constellation
when God hid their words
    in the wind's voices, limiting
       their pitch to whispers of leaves.

Did the starry-eyed people of Shinar climb
to topple God, or simply to ask:
Teach us the plenitude of living invisibly,
of rushing through as water or wind.
Teach us when to return, startled,
    to the outer limits of air.

EMILY WARN is the author of *The Leaf Path* (Copper Canyon Press) and two poetry chapbooks, *The Book of Esther* (Jugum Press) and *Highway Street* (Limberlost Press). A graduate of Kalamazoo College and the University of Washington, she recently held a Stegner Fellowship at Stanford University and currently lives in Seattle, Washington. Her poems and poetry reviews have appeared in *The Seattle Times, The Bloomsbury Review, The Kenyon Review,* and *Parabola*.

BOOK DESIGN and composition by John D. Berry and Jennifer Van West, using Adobe PageMaker 6.0 on a Macintosh IIvx and a Power 120. The type is Scala, a humanist typeface with an open character shape designed by Martin Majoor. Scala was created in 1988 for the printed matter of the *Muziekcentrum Vredenburg* in Utrecht, in the Netherlands, and released by FontShop International in 1991 as part of the FontFont series of digital typefaces. *Printed by McNaughton & Gunn.*